Who Would Not Want An Inheritance?

Stephen Meiner

Published by Stephen Meiner, 2024.

This is a work of fiction. Similarities to real people, places, or events are entirely coincidental.

WHO WOULD NOT WANT AN INHERITANCE?

First edition. March 26, 2024.

Copyright © 2024 Stephen Meiner.

ISBN: 979-8224516704

Written by Stephen Meiner.

There are scams out there ...and I've heard so many stories.

I once got an email from an individual who said his country was under siege, and he saw on social media that I am a Christian. He said he is a Christian too ...and by reading my posts, he said he could tell I was a good person. And you guessed it ...he wanted to send me his money because if the coup was successful he could in no way trust the new government. He was afraid they'd use his money for evil means.

At what point does this seem 'not quite right'?

Well, right from the start.

I decided to have some fun with this. I emailed him back, and said I didn't trust my government either. I suggested he transfer his wealth into diamonds and send it to my post office box.

At this point, I don't want the IRS to get excited ...it was just a joke. You know ...like this is not serious. You recognize this as a scam, right? And I'm just trying to amuse myself ...it seems like I seldom amuse anyone else.

If I've failed so far ...what else is new!!

2

But, if you are still with me, I will begin my real story.

Well, it is not really *my* story ...but it is *real*.

I.

The Pastor of the church I go to says he has many friends ...and in truth, I've seen these friends, and some of them are my friends too. Though there are those he says are his friends ...and he mentions that he has never met them, but sometimes there are ways we can know a person we have never met. And we can know they are ...*a friend*.

Yes, we can begin to know a person we have never met—-by reading about them, or by what they've written—-and most of the time we are not privileged to have an occasion to meet them, so they don't know us. But, you can read about someone who does know you. And of course, you have probably guessed by now that I'm talking about a *friendship* ...or you may refer to it as a *relationship* with Jesus.

Pastor Tom tells great stories, gives great messages. He also plays the guitar and sings ...and does all things well, in my opinion.

The Associate Pastor is one of my dearest friends too. We share jokes, a bit of wisdom at times ...and oh yes, we also share a fondness for chocolate.

We share our faith openly, but we share chocolate mostly in private. Though I think Myron's wife knows, so it's no secret.

II.

Our belief in God should not be a secret.

First, I'd like to address the issue that I first mentioned.

'To come into money' is to suddenly become rich (or richer than we were) through no action or effort on our part. Usually it refers to an inheritance ...as someone in your family dies, and there is a legal document or will.

They say, "Where there's a will, there's a way!" And hopefully the way you got the inheritance was not by hastening the process ...by feeding the elderly relative too much chocolate.

You can also come into money by winning the lottery. That may be one of the most surprising and electrifying experiences ...but so is any occasion of being struck by lightning, and the chances of that are probably higher.

Or you can get money from a lawsuit. Someone recently tried to sue a family member. It was not a direct family member ...as none of us have any money, so there would be no point. And I believe the point of a lawsuit against someone is usually a bit corrupt anyway. Those being sued can usually afford being sued. Those with money who do things that would make you want to sue them, if they just changed their ways, I think that would be all around better. I don't want their money.

Each of us is different, and it depends on the person ...but, would you rather 'come into money' by means of winning the lottery or by inheriting money from a loved one? And just to make it fair ...let's say that both amounts would be the same.

Now, if multiple people are involved with not everyone getting the same amount of winnings—-or multiple people inherit, yet some get more than others—-then that can get a bit tense and uncomfortable.

That leads to my next point.

The most valuable thing you can leave your children is not money.

III.

Where did this idea of 'first-born' and birthright come from??

Perhaps you can answer that better than I can ...but, while reading the Bible, we read about it for the first time before God says it's what they are to do.

The *'law'* was given to Moses to write down to give to the people after they fled Egypt. And that was after Abraham—-Isaac—-Jacob—-to even after that time Joseph interpreted Pharaoh's dream, predicting a famine. And when the famine hit, all of Joseph's large extended family went to Egypt. Yet, when that particular Pharaoh died, the new leadership was not at all kind. And God had Moses lead them out of Egypt.

I didn't live back then, so I couldn't email them my post office box address. Anyway, that wouldn't have worked. Their wealth was likely not in diamonds ...but in cows. Well, I tried to milk that for all it's worth ...let's moo-ve on.

Since the *law given to Moses for the people* had not been written yet, Where did their previous practice come from?

I don't know.

You may say, "You are writing a book, and you say you don't know?"

Well, I've been told it is more acceptable to say, "I don't know!" than to claim to know something you don't know.

And you may say, "Well, yes, I agree ...but those people aren't writing a book about something they don't know about."

Fair point.

I do believe those who write textbooks about 'evolution' ...are doing that very thing, yet this time the question is "What do I know?"

Let me mention something I do know then.

I do know that while Abraham was still named Abram, there was a famine in the land. And if you want to check me on it, it is in the 12th Chapter of the Book of Genesis ...and I know many people like to fact-check nowadays. It's right there, unless ...no, I don't think (AI) Artificial Intelligence has gotten their hands on your Bible (yet), so it should be right there.

Anyway, there was a great famine in the land and Abram took his wife with him to Egypt, yet didn't tell them she was his wife. You can read about that, but the short of it ...is that God plagued Pharaoh and his house. And Pharaoh asked why Abram didn't tell him it was his wife.

In Chapter 20, Abraham journeyed with Sarah again ...this time to Gerar, where Abimelech was the Philistine king. And again, Abraham doesn't say she is his wife. This time God tells Abimelech, *"Behold, you are a dead man ..."* And then Abimelech called together all his servants, and told them ...and they were all afraid.

In Chapter 26, Abraham's son Isaac takes Rebekah, his wife, with him to Gerar ...yet, also did as his dad had done and told them it was his sister. Abimelech looks out a window and sees them playfully acting much unlike brother and sister. He then confronts Isaac, yet tells all his own people, *"He that touches this man or his wife shall surely be put to death."*

It should be noted that though they did not follow God, both the Pharaoh in Egypt and the Philistine king Abimelech feared God. Strange, isn't it, that many people today say there is no evidence for God's existence ...yet, these people would have definitely disagreed with that claim.

No, I haven't forgotten. My thoughts are still on the 'birthright' ...and that means I have to back up one Chapter, to Genesis 25.

IV.

Genesis 25: 21 & 22 ...two people pray to God, for two different reasons.

In verse 21, Isaac prays to God because his wife wasn't becoming pregnant ...and he wanted her to.

In verse 22, Rebekah prays because it was a difficult pregnancy ...and she asked God why. Obviously, Isaac's prayer had been answered, and now she was seeking an answer also ...not asking why she was pregnant, like I said, that was obvious. She was asking why it was so difficult.

And God answered her, stating that two nations were in her womb, two manner of people, and the elder son shall serve the younger.

Now, it is difficult to make a real issue about who is the eldest ...since they were born on the same day, within the same hour, nearly at the same time. As the first son was born, the hand of the second son had a grasp on the first son's heel as he was being (delivered) born.

The first son was named Esau, meaning 'hairy' ...because he was.

Their second son was named Jacob, meaning 'seize by the heel' ...because he was doing that.

Mostly today, I hear that Jacob means supplanter ...a word most people don't use. But, there is a word that people are way more familiar with ...which they seem often too eager to use, and that word is 'deceiver'.

Now, through my life ...well, of all the sports, I have followed football (not soccer, but the NFL) more than any other sport. And I would say that Tom Brady was the best quarterback to ever play the game. The word 'goat' wasn't always a compliment. It used to mean someone was the cause or blame for something going wrong. Years ago, it was not good to be called a goat. But, today G.O.A.T. means, *Greatest Of All Time* ...and I'd say Tom Brady should at least be considered as the G.O.A.T. football player.

When someone wins time and again, fans of other teams get tired of it, and they have a different way of viewing it ...and they are more inclined to be hypercritical and harsh to the point of perhaps not being fair about it. When someone is successful, do we feel they get unfair advantages or treatment??

Well, I've heard people call Tom Brady ...'cheater'. And I imagine there was a point when Esau might have been inclined to call his brother 'deceiver'. Yet, I cannot imagine any Mom calling her adorable newborn 'deceiver'. Jacob was named for what he was doing—-'seizing the heel'. Or is it possible that she perhaps looked at what God had told her ...that Jacob was 'to take the place of' his older brother (who was older perhaps by a few seconds) ...and that would also reference the 'birthright'??

V.

The 'birthright' had a twofold meaning. The firstborn was to inherit a double portion of his father's possessions ...and he was to become the leader of the family.

Now, where did this idea of firstborn 'birthright' come from?

Again, I say, "I don't know."

But I did mention that Abraham went to Egypt, and then to the Philistine city of Gerar. And Isaac also went to Gerar. And it seems like God's people often looked to other nations and how they did things. God never wanted them to have kings, but they persisted and hundreds of years later they got King Saul ...King David ...then King Solomon.

Of course, the kings of Israel were much after the law which God gave to Moses. But, Abraham did not give the birthright to the firstborn, neither did Jacob give such a blessing to his firstborn, Reuben. Even after the law given to Moses, that protocol was not followed in anointing the kings. King David was the youngest of eight sons, and Solomon was not David's first son ...not even of his first wife.

So, why is it that Isaac was going to follow the 'birthright' ...and why was it such a big thing, when it wasn't even written down as a standard until Moses came hundreds of years later??

Maybe we can look beyond Jacob getting the 'birthright' to the time Jacob got old and prepared to bless his sons. Not his firstborn, but his son who is in the genealogy of the line of Jesus ...Judah, also had a mindset for standards that were not yet established. It seems some standards had good intentions, yet other standards appear to me as having been simply terrible. Sorry, but I jump around a lot ...that's just how my brain works. And I am in Chapter 38 now ...with Judah marrying and having three sons.

I think it's a bit strange, but I understand it ...and it is the part that seems to have good intentions. Tamar married Judah's oldest son, and when her husband died, Judah told the next oldest son to marry her to 'raise up an inheritance' for her. Actually, the Bible says Judah referred to it as to raise up an heir to your (dead) brother. It actually seemed like an honorable way to take care of the widows who would otherwise possibly be without.

Yet, Judah's second son also died after marrying Tamar. Having lost two sons now, understandably he would not be able to get beyond the grief ...and he may have been thinking Tamar was going to 'do in' his third son also, so I can see his hesitation with following their standard of doing things (wherever that came from). But, we know from the Bible that it was not Tamar's fault ...it says that God had them die.

So often we take things into our own hands when things seem to be going wrong for us. And as we often do, the people we read about in the Bible also did. Tamar decided to do something about it when

Judah failed to keep his promise. She put a veil over her face and tricked Judah.

Judah's response to seeing that Tamar was pregnant, not knowing that it was by him, was to have her be burned to death.

Now, where did Judah get that from?

It was still hundreds of years before the law was established by God and given to Moses, and though it was strict—-it was not as strict as what was being called for at this moment, and God's way would hold both the man and woman responsible. Judah was guilty, and he was not considering any punishment for himself.

So, where did this pretense of justice come from?

Again, I don't know ...yet, my guess would be from other nations. And we saw how they spent a significant amount of time living among other people. I've read somewhere (sorry, I can't footnote the source) that Egypt burned people ...maybe that's not accurate, so sorry again. I can say 'sorry' twice, right? After all, this does involve 'apologetics'.

What we do know is that somehow the notion of punishment for when a woman becomes pregnant outside of marriage is often argued with a very strong bias, not considering as much *how* she became pregnant ... and in this case, *not* including the misdeeds of Judah.

Adultery is often branded as solely a woman's sin ...and I've heard Christians say that adultery is punishable in the Bible, but not fornication. Pointing out that Judah's wife had died and Tamar's husband had died ...neither of them were married, so it wasn't adultery. Yet, Judah called for Tamar to be burned to death.

When Jesus came, He said that the one without sin should cast the first stone. They were trying to catch Jesus on a law they never really followed. If they didn't catch the woman in the act, how could they convict her? And stupidly, they insisted she be stoned because they *did* catch her in the act—-though they never intended to do anything to the man—-to which they had just confessed they had caught also.

But, back to Judah ...I don't know where he got that, I just know he didn't get it from God. And when Tamar showed the signet, bracelets, and staff to be Judah's ...well, it seems things were okay again, and no need for anyone to become alarmed.

And an additional note: Tamar is listed along with Judah in the genealogy, in the line of Jesus.

VI.

I gave fair warning that I jump around a lot ...yet, there is so much to say about all this, and I can't say it all at once.

The 'birthright' had a rather high value placed upon it. And most people think a double portion is a good thing. Isaac and I have at least one thing in common ...we both like venison. And I like when I get a double portion. That doesn't mean I want more than someone else ...and I don't like to think someone gets less because I get more. I just like to think someone doesn't like venison as much as me ...and when they take all they want, I'm happy for the leftovers that no one else wants.

My dad also served wild turkeys for Thanksgiving...yes, I'm talking about the bird. My mom also cooked a turkey from the store. There was a definite difference in taste. Most everyone was used to the turkey bought at the store ...but, the one my dad shot had a wilder taste. I heard the comment, "That's too 'gamey' for me!"

Dad and I ate the wild turkey and the others mostly ate the one from the store.

Deer can have a wide variation in taste also. A big buck often doesn't taste as good. And there is a big difference in taste depending on whether the deer ate mostly from a corn field, or whether it was a swamp buck. Swamp bucks often ate the low branches of cedar trees, as far as their necks could reach. And that's the kind of venison I like ...'gamey'.

Isaac liked his venison ...and he told Esau, *"Behold, I am old. I know not the day of my death ...go out to the field, and take me some venison; and make me savory meat such that I love, and bring it to me that I may eat; that my soul may bless you before I die."* (Chapter 27 of Genesis, and that's not referencing the musical group.)

The first verse of that Chapter says that Isaac cannot see ...and in verse four, he says "before I die." Well, Isaac lived approximately 20 more years. It reminds me of Fred Sanford placing his hand over his heart and saying, "Oh, this is the big one!"

Venison is my favorite meat, but I would never hold my hand to my chest and say, "Quick, go get me some venison ...I think this may be the big one!"

But, Isaac did tell his son, Esau, to go get some venison for him to eat—-and he implied that he may die soon. And Rebekah heard this also—-so, wouldn't they both believe this would be the time, by Isaac's own words—-that this was going to be the time of the 'birthright' blessing??

How would it *not* be precisely as Isaac said ...not the precise moment of his death, but the precise moment of the blessing??

God knew what Rebekah would do, and she was actually doing what she was told by God would happen, but she hadn't been told *how* it would happen or *when* ...but she realized at this moment that the *'when'* was now!!

God had said it would happen ...and God always knows how things will happen and when. God is never surprised.

When we are not certain how things are going to work out in our lives, we often mess up. And God knows that we often have to mess up before we become as committed as we should be.

VII.

It seems that Isaac and Rebekah saw the 'birthright' differently ...as did Esau and Jacob.

Perhaps Esau and Jacob saw it much the same ...something valuable to attain. But, Esau had it all wrong ...and Jacob didn't realize, it seemed, that he was on course for the right part.

It seemed only Rebekah understood what she deemed as the critical part ...as God had answered her request to Him to tell her the reason for her discomfort during her pregnancy. But, likely she was feeling even more discomfort at this moment. The end of Chapter 26 speaks largely of what the problem was ...Esau had two wives who were both *'a grief of mind'* to Isaac and Rebekah.

In Chapter 27, verse 35, Isaac took the role of the reluctant father, and told Esau that his brother had stolen his blessing. And after much anguish, in verse 41, Esau says he wants to kill his brother.

Rebekah tells Jacob he had better run ...and Jacob can find refuge far away, with her own brother.

So, the part of the 'birthright' where one gets a double portion did not seem forthcoming for Jacob, as he was fleeing all the possessions.

That would make it easier on Esau who likely valued the possessions more. Yet the more important part of the 'birthright' should have been the leadership part—-which Esau had already failed miserably on, and which Jacob was not prepared for, but he would be.

It would be some tough lessons, but Jacob had the start in his heart. And God was about to send him through 'boot camp' to ready him for who he needed to be ...to be the *'leader'*.

And the best leaders are the ones *who can follow* the ones they should follow.

Yet, often much else has to be learned. And we have a tendency to half-commit to things.

Not an easy lesson, but more fully committing to something often comes after feeling the pain of our failures.

There is another truth to be seen here also. Others often trust they can have success when they see how others have struggled and overcome their hardships. Hope often comes from feeling you are not alone, and seeing what others have done ...believing perhaps you can do it too.

VIII.

I've often heard people say, "You don't know what it's like."

And on most occasions, they are right in saying that.

I worked in a mental health prison. There was a person who was there who'd been born a girl, yet was having extensive operations and treatment to try to become a male. She was nearing the end of her transition when she trashed that medical facility.

Why did she begin destroying the place that was helping her become who she felt she wanted to be?

Well, again ...you can see here on record that I am once again saying I don't really know. But, I do know her Dad was in the military ...and I can't remember if he was a Navy Seal, or not. Yet, he was very much committed to what he was doing for his country. And what child would not have admiration for that!! Yet, that same child may wonder if they are admired in return. Or at least acknowledged as being special, after all ...they *are* the person's own child.

One of the strongest emotions is the desire to be accepted. And that can make all the difference. It can either inspire or destroy.

And how often does a person primarily seek approval from the one in their life they don't get it from?

I admit that I don't know if it was the case here, but how many times do we hear of someone trying desperately to relate to one of their parents??

I think we have at least some evidence of this with both Jacob and Esau.

Yet, sometimes it's not that. Sometimes it's something else entirely that a person is struggling with. And often we are just guessing ...and sometimes tragically guessing wrong. If the person tells me, "You don't know what it's like!" ...they are right, I don't.

But, though they may be right that I don't know how it is to *feel* a certain way, they may be very wrong to say I don't know *what is right*.

I always hesitate to drop names, especially without permission, but since this person has been attempting to communicate her *feelings* on the subject of something that went very wrong—-well, I feel rather confident that she would want the word to get out to as many people as possible, especially since there is so much censorship to prevent this kind of testimony. And though I don't know how people feel, as I'll always admit, I know Chloe Cole does know how it feels. And if you care enough, you will look up her name ...and you can see what she says about it.

Sadly, people seem to have to go through things before the terrible wrongs in a society are addressed. And even more sad is the fact that when those things do come out, they find little support from society.

I entered college in 1973, with the drinking age at 18 years of age in Michigan and over half of the other states in the nation. I was surprised to read that the United States was third in the world for the number of universities within their country, yet our nation still prides themselves with arguably having 8 out of 10 of the most prestigious institutions of *'higher learning'*. The point is that the US has lots of young adults going to college. In 1984, Congress passed the Uniform Minimum Drinking Age Act—-establishing 21 years of age as the legal age for purchasing alcohol.

Why did it take so long to realize that when you take a campus full of virtually unsupervised hormonal college kids—-and add the indiscretion of alcohol—-that there is not much *'higher learning'* going on?? But, they did eventually address it to a certain extent.

I'm glad the drinking age is 21 years of age. But, why are we wise enough to say they can't go to a bar until the age of 21, but we can send them to a butcher as young as 13 years of age??

Yet, though society may fail us ...we can still help each other. And my heart goes out to those like Chloe—-who is attempting to reach others with her heart, wanting to truly help those—-who people like me would never be able to help.

Who'd listen to me?

You don't need to listen to me.

Listen to Chloe ...she cares.

I care too ...but, she understands.

If you have a drinking problem, go to Al-Anon ...don't come to me. People have said I'm more qualified to be Q-Anon.

Of course, I disagree ...but, likely you are not going to go to a source that you don't trust. Often people don't trust someone who hasn't gone through the struggle ...and are not ready to put their confidence in the claims of one who has not experienced it.

The source that I trust is the Bible. The Bible often doesn't paint a pretty picture ...it tells it how it is. And it tells of a Savior, who was crucified by those who did not like the fact that others were listening to Him, instead of them.

IX.

To have faith in God, I'd say it's rather important to know who God is.

We don't know what Isaac and Rebekah had told their two sons. We don't know how much they paid attention either.

We do know much of what was known at that time came through someone verbally telling them. We don't know how they retained the information, nor do we know if they were given a slanted version of what they did retain ...so, the truth may have been difficult.

I'm glad God didn't have Moses wander idly in the desert for 40 years after they were led out of Egypt. God had Moses write it all down, the correct information, with the perfect description of what we all need to know. And I don't need to retain the information ...because I can reread it at any time.

But, Moses wasn't there yet, to write what God wanted them to know ...so, often learning the hard way was what they had to do. I consider reading of their struggles and learning from them as a huge benefit to us. Those who learned it the hard way likely learned it better ...and perhaps we can trust them, having more confidence in listening to them.

As is always the case, everybody has an opinion. And we don't only hear one side of the story (they hadn't created a monopoly with social media and the news networks yet back then). And Esau and Jacob likely heard the stories from various individuals, just like Isaac and Rebekah would have.

Let me have a little fun here (as if I haven't already taken that liberty), and let's say Esau and Jacob had a friend 'Al'. My keyboard types (AI) Artificial Intelligence the same way that it types 'Al' ...as in Allen, Albert, or Alex. But, I knew that ...and that's where I'm having my fun. Suppose their friend Al tells them what his parents shared with him about God.

So, their fictitious friend Al says, "Oh, wasn't that special ...they started out in a sort of paradise, then they ate a fruit they weren't supposed to and got kicked out of that garden paradise. Then we don't know much about what happened after that, other than it got real bad and God killed everybody, except a family of eight were spared. Everyone else died in a flood that covered the entire earth. Then everyone chipped in to build a tower to at least be protected from the possibility of smaller floods that may be forthcoming, but God destroyed the tower and confused everyone's language. Then when people started to get settled, God told some people to move far away ...which they did, because God said so."

"My Dad says that all the time."

"He says what?"

"He says, 'Because I said so!' Oh ...but that's not all."

"Your dad says more than that?"

"No ...well, yes, my dad talks all the time, but I'm talking about God. After God tells them to move far away, and they go to a strange place and try to make a go of it, God decides to destroy one of the cities my dad's cousin was living in."

"How bad was it?"

"How bad is 'destroy'? The entire city and its inhabitants went up in smoke ...though dad's cousin and his family escaped first."

"Yeh, that's right ...and they were told not to glance back."

Now, viewing this conversation ...one could get an entirely different impression of how things were. Yet, like I said earlier, I am so glad God had Moses write it down so we can understand that God never intended for things to be this way ...but, He did intend for us to have the freedom of choice. And that seems to be what the whole world wants ...and it's especially true of those who don't have many freedoms.

And it's also likely true why in areas with little freedom so many people embrace the choice to accept the truth about Jesus. They often know more clearly what is right & wrong than nations which have the most freedoms, also considering themselves the most advanced and civilized (like the nation I live in); and often these supposedly uncivilized people seek out what is good in their heart. Though they may not see the good around them, they know there is such a thing as good ...and that they have not been doing it. Yet, they can recognize the joy of those telling them ...when Jesus is revealed to them. And very often they want that joy too.

If I were going to share the truth with those hungry for the truth, it would not be to give them the 'knowledge of good & evil' ...they have likely already experienced the evil. They are waiting for the good.

But, for those who have viewed good to be inclusive of all—-what I'm saying is that salvation can be inclusive of all people who come to Him—-as God would have it that none would perish. God said He would have spared Sodom if there were ten righteous people living there. Yes, God wants to include all people, but not all behaviors.

And why can't all behaviors be included?

Well, that was tried, and it failed miserably.

Was God surprised when that happened?

No.

It's a bit confusing, but God created the angels first ...and it was some sort of paradise we cannot imagine. But, it was not a paradise for robots ...it was for those who have freedom of choice, in the first case, the angels.

Yet, God knew it would not only fail, but that it would become very bad ...with the worst imagined evil somehow coming forth.

Galatians 5:9 speaks not only to us, it was so true for the angels also. *"A little leaven ...leavens the whole lump."*

Thankfully for the sake of two-thirds of the angels, they decided not to lump themselves with the other third. Yet, even with a two-to-one ratio advantage, there was no stopping it ...unless God got involved.

And He did.

It is what I believe we read about in the first verse of the Bible, after God quelled the rebellion. Even the two-thirds angels likely didn't know what had happened at that point.

And there was no singing ...yet.

The two-thirds angels began singing at Creation, as I perceive it.

And God put a man in a garden paradise, then also gave him a woman ...but knew they would both be tempted.

At the time of Noah, God said, *"every imagination of the thoughts of his (the human's) heart was only evil continually."*

So, two virtual paradises lost ...so, is anyone placing their bets on how it would be a third time around??

Why will Heaven be any different??

God will not do a frontal lobotomy on us as we enter the afterlife. So, how can we know that our promised heavenly paradise will not be destroyed also ...by the existence of our freedom of choice??

Well, our freedom of choice is too often made here on earth amid much deception and temptation, as it was in the Garden of Eden. And that will not be the case in Heaven.

And all of those who'd joined to side with the violent rebellion within the heavens, making up the *third*, well, that third has already chosen to have their membership somewhere else. And they'll likely expect their cronies to join them in their *highly* exclusive club.

Or would that be *lowly* ...or lower than low.

X.

Yet, back to Jacob and Esau. I believe their choices in life were a bit more clear …maybe not easier, but more clear.

I don't believe the lines of *right & wrong* had been blurred as they have been today, especially with us 'civilized' people.

Even Pharaoh's nation and the king of the Philistines had a better sense of right and wrong. They somehow felt it didn't apply to them, yet they respected what was held 'right' by others …and *feared God*.

So, in *that way*, they had better understanding than many of us.

God promises us an eternity of peace with Him …without Him, there would be no peace at all. And God will deliver on that promise.

But, the *guarantee of our peaceful life* with Him means there will have to be a separation from those who would make it not so.

It was made very unpeaceful in the past, and it would happen again, but God promises that it won't. He allows us the freedom here on earth to choose who we want to be in charge …and He doesn't insist that it is Him that we choose.

So, the leader is important. But, with God there will not be multiple leaders, nor will the leadership change. Those who accept God as their leader, and want Him in charge ...will have that very promised peace with Him.

And God hates the behavior that leads to that which totally disrupts and corrupts that peace.

Malachi 1:2-3 reads, *"I have loved you, says the LORD. Yet, you say, wherein have you loved us? Was not Esau ...Jacob's brother? says the LORD, yet I loved Jacob. And I hated Esau ..."*

Some people say that verse is very confusing, and I am making it even more confusing, as perhaps the confusing point was not even thought of ...until I brought it up.

Some people like *'detail'*, and want more ...while others say, "Too much detail." As you can guess, I get that a lot.

We get distinct impressions by: what we read, what others say, what we experience, and what we think ...as the impressions build upon past impressions, usually in the same direction as in the past.

Nowadays it is often summed up by saying everyone is different, and we are all just 'wired' slightly different. Most people would not have a problem with that statement, but how do we view God?

God is the same always, and He loves us all the same ...yet, in truth, God doesn't want us to live the same lives that He knows will '*leaven the whole lump*.'

If we feel we have it somewhat good, there are others who do not. There has never been a time in our human lives where evil did not exist ...somewhere.

And the 'somewhere' could become 'anywhere', and it could visit any of us anytime—-and it visits often in some people's lives—-those lives that God loves. And God hates the choices made that lead to that which causes us so much pain.

Many of the choices that Jacob made would not be pleasing to many of us, but God sees the person and the direction. God was working to redeem Jacob's life.

XI.

But, why wasn't it working also with Esau's life?

Perhaps it is because Esau felt a false sense of security ...knowing he was in good with his dad, over things that had much less value. Yet, in the back of his mind he knew he was not pleasing God.

And often we think too strictly of God, and think we've messed up so much that God will not forgive us. I've heard that from people way too many times.

In all honesty, if I heard it just one time ...it would be too many times.

If we embrace the love of Jesus, we can separate ourselves from the past, and not look at ourselves fully in view of our behavior. But, if we don't understand God's love ...we often *become the behavior*, and the behavior tends to get worse.

So, when it is said that God hated Esau ...the way I see it, God hated who Esau became ...God hated the behavior.

Why is God's hate so important to understand? Because God loves us, and He hates what gets in the way of that.

God also knows how much it hurts us ...and how it often leads us through self-condemnation, or sometimes guilt festers within us. And it blocks future avenues for reconciliation.

XII.

As I read again through the life of Jacob and Esau ...there is so much to learn from the life of Jacob. Yet, I also see many occasions of guidance and circumstances created by a loving God to bring Esau where he needed to be also.

Often we look for the little things that give us a false sense of security; often settling for the comfort that comes from how we feel our friends and family view us. No one I know likes to be hated, so each little bit of encouragement is important. And there is something to be said for the statement, *"It's the little things in life which are important."* If we expect too much, it is true that we can miss the little things that are happening to guide us along the way. Eventually, it would be best if everyone would be guided along the way ...by *the Way, the Truth, and the Life.*

But, what happens with those we know who don't have much depth of understanding about God?

Well, the lives of each and every one of us—-do we think those in our lives, or those we are yet to meet—-that they do *not* come into our lives for a reason?

And sometimes we are not to move on, until those very reasons are fulfilled. The difficulty is when we have no clue as to why things are happening ...and it very much complicates our understanding of it, and the mood and motivation we bring to each day.

Esau didn't seem nearly as concerned with pleasing his dad until he was facing grave disappointment, and he felt let down.

In Genesis 28:6-9, when Esau's dad blessed his brother and told him not to marry a Canaanite woman, it seemed that Esau suddenly wanted to please his dad ...and likewise chose not to go to the Canaanite women. This was certainly a change from two Chapters earlier when he was *a grief of mind unto Isaac and Rebekah*.

Was there hope for Esau?

Of course ...there is hope for all of us!!

XIII.

Having secured the blessing from his dad, how was Jacob now doing?

How was that working for him?

Jacob was very distraught. It was not easy trying to deal with his uncle ...especially with trying to arrange a marriage with Laban's daughter.

After having received the 'birthright' blessing from his dad, why was he in a land far away from his dad? And any blessing he felt he could have was no more than fleeting expectations laced with false hopes, now more increasingly difficult to deal with.

What was Jacob to do? He didn't have a can of spinach to help him get through the intolerable moments. What was it that Popeye said? *"That's all I can stands, I can't stands no more!"*

But Jacob didn't tell Laban to 'can it!'

Jacob did get his uncle's two daughters as his wives ...and plenty of children. You can read about that in Chapters 29 & 30.

Still no spinach, Jacob was learning how to cope with life. Yet, he needed help. In verse 13 of Chapter 31, God tells Jacob to leave with his family and return back home.

Chapter 32 tells how Jacob is going to do as God directed him to do, but though he was going to do it ...it was not easy for Jacob. He still fears Esau.

As Jacob anticipates meeting his brother, during that night he wrestles his fears and anxiety ...then actually physically wrestles with whom he perceives is an angel. Jacob persists to wrestle, saying he won't let go until he is given a blessing.

Now, how is that? Hadn't he already received the blessing from his dad? Yes, that was approximately 20 years ago, but it is a moment he would never forget ...and it is clear in his mind. It was the blessing that seemed to begin the process of questioning whether he was blessed at all. When we don't really feel something, we question it, and we seek out constant affirmation.

And the 'birthright' blessing he had received those many years ago hadn't given him a double-portion ...he felt he had no portion.

Or he could conclude he had a double-portion of problems. And it was going to get worse ...he was about to meet up with his brother again.

Whoever Jacob perceives he is wrestling with throughout the night does bless him, and Jacob says, *"...my life is preserved."*

Though often saying something doesn't make it true ...unless God says it, and Jacob didn't understand all that yet.

We see this in Chapter 33, where Jacob has his wives and children go first, and then it was Jacob's turn to step up in verse 3: *"...bowing himself to the ground seven times, until he came near his brother."*

Verse 4, shows us the response that Jacob received ...which he surely did not expect from his brother. Esau ran to meet him, embraced him, and kissed him (in the brotherly fashion).

Then they both cried.

Part of the drama leading up to this, besides all the bowing on Jacob's part, involved Jacob offering Esau a gift. Now we get Esau's response: *"I have enough, my brother; keep for yourself what you have."*

Esau must have been feeling good and confident at this point. He had not desired so much a true blessing from God, but from his dad. And Esau now appeared content with the way things were.

Each person's blessings from God cannot be merely passed on from person-to-person ...it must come from God, and each person must decide whether to accept it.

But families can help us out in big ways also ...by loving us. The very sad part of that is when the family doesn't know how to show it, or if it is perhaps not seen as love. Though sadder still, and tragic ...is when there is not love.

Esau desired possessions, and he had possessions. That is not love, yet some people perceive it that way.

The part of the 'birthright' besides the possessions ...was supposed to involve naming the eldest as the leader of the family. And when Jacob bowed to Esau, perhaps that fed that portion of the unfulfilled desire Esau had. In verse 12 of Chapter 33, Esau enthusiastically tells his brother that he will lead the way ...but Jacob declines.

Jacob may not have always been so confident with his relationship with God, but there was enough there that he knew he couldn't be led by both God and his brother.

In Chapter 35, God tells Jacob to go to the place where he'd first fled from his brother. The past is often difficult to deal with. And even when the present appears to be uncharacteristically rosy, the old feelings—-that things could always change quickly back to the way they were—-is a feeling not easy to rid ourselves of. We may need something to replace those old feelings.

God addresses Jacob and directs him to build an altar. At this point, Jacob doesn't want a mixed blessing, or one he could be totally deprived of, so Jacob tells all those with him to gather all their trinkets, earrings, and foreign idols ...and he gets rid of them.

Nearing the end of Chapter 35, Jacob finally comes to his dad. And the last verse says that Isaac died ...and Esau and Jacob buried him.

It doesn't mention Rebekah, but it seems at this point the parental window is closed, and each has to go the way of their own choosing. No more faint view of whether dad or mom approves, supports, or encourages.

Esau and Jacob were both highly influenced by their parents ...and most of the time we are too.

I got a wholesome and moral upbringing. Dad & Mom were both a continual blessing to all of us six children ...but as Dad often said about other things, *Things were different in my day!*

XIV.

One noteworthy thing I want to mention here:

After Jacob and his family travel to Egypt (yes, another famine), they are living in favor. But, leadership in nations can change ...and it did change. They began living in servitude ...and all newborn males were to be drowned in the Nile.

I'm trying to stay in the Book of Genesis, but it is so very interesting, I cannot *not* also encourage you to read about what is described in the Book of Exodus, beginning in Chapter two. I'm not listing it here because you should read it for yourself.

Anyway, later God directs Moses to lead them out of Egypt. And what God has Moses write down—-for the standard for His people to live by, at that time—-includes a first-born *'birthright'.*

If it was for the most part seldom followed, then why would it ever be considered such a firm standard?

And why did God focus on what Egypt and other nations seemed to so highly esteem?

God's wisdom is supreme, not borrowed. And it doesn't seem like those who followed it were people who were following God?

So, why did God put forth something that His people so often made exception to? What is the wisdom, or value in that!?!

This time I'm not saying, "I don't know." I'll try to explain.

There is a strong influence of the 'first-born'. Not across families, but within families ...the younger ones most of the time look up to their older siblings.

What better way to encourage our other children, than to encourage the 'first-born'!! And it is often more difficult for the 'first-born' within a family ...because they don't often see how others have dealt with what they are encountering. They struggle through it themselves in many ways, but the struggle does not have to be so much a struggle if we as parents are sensitive to what they are going through and just encourage them along.

Then, it is sort of like what I mentioned in my Chapter VIII; a few pages back ...where the one struggling with alcohol turns to a group where people share that struggle. And likewise, the children may not relate so much to a dad who says, *"Things were a lot different in my day."* And that is kind of implying that dad doesn't really understand. But, the younger siblings feel the older sibling does understand.

The oldest child is also often a bit of a challenge for the parents also. Since it is their 'first-born' ...they have not raised any children before. This child is their first ...and much of it can be modeled after what their parents had done. But, considering there may just be a bit of truth in the saying, *"Things were a lot different in my day!"* ...well, if that's true, then what worked back then may not be the thing to do today.

But, if we parents are open to their needs, and sensitive to their sensitivities ...then we may have a huge blessing of our own by putting a little more effort into guiding the 'first-born', who may later help guide the rest of our children in a good way. Yet, we should also seek out the hearts of the younger ones ...making it clear there is not a favored child.

Did God show me this? Well, I do try to understand what I read.

Do you know what? Everything in the Bible is what God wants me to know. Yet, I never fully understand some things ...and other things are not clear at all. Should I just give up trying to understand?

No, I'll not give up. The Bible is God's Word ...and what is there is there to help me. And God loves us. I should at least know *that.*

And He wants you to know it too.

XV.

I have a tendency to get carried away.

But, God knows my heart ..and God often carries me.

I'm attending a Bible study on Wednesday evenings ...at the church that I go to on Sundays also.

The Pastor's wife is a real good cook, and they set out a table of desserts, fruits, and vegetables. Many other wonderful ladies (and some men) also bring food. I'd like to thank them all, but I'm not good with names. I mostly only remember faces—-and when they are carrying food—-I only see the food they are carrying. No one has brought venison or wild turkey yet.

The past two studies were by Max Lucado ...study booklets, and a video to go along with it. The first one was: *'Help Is Here'*

The study we just started last week is: *'God Never Gives Up On You'*

Max is one of those friends you have ...who you have never met in person, yet you know the 'person' because of what he writes. Isn't that how we get to know about God better ...by reading God's Word?

That's the kind of friend Max is to Pastor Tom ...who has chosen several of Max's studies now. Yes, what was the title of that other one? It should be right there with my other books, but I can't find it. "Probably right there under my nose ...could probably find it if I'd not be so anxious." That's what the title was: *'Anxious for Nothing'*

Max's books were a dear friend to our five children. We read them the book, *'Tell Me the Secrets: Treasures for Eternity'*—-and they were so good that we also bought some of the stories within that story with great illustrations to go along with it. And anyone who does well by my children is a friend of mine too.

Now, I'd like to explain something about me 'getting carried away'.

In Max's study guide book there are spaces to write answers to questions which Max asks for his study format. And since Max leaves blank spaces for us to write in our comments and thoughts, then I think it's only fair if I'm participating in the study, that I have adequate space for my thoughts.

But, I did not.

So, instead ...this book provides the space. And that's what I mean by getting carried away. We haven't even reached the second week of our study ...and here I am.

I'm not entering the ring to spar with heavyweights like Max Lucado or Josh McDowell (it would be ridiculous in my mind, to try to put my writing next to them, and I wouldn't want to be a 'grief of mind' to anyone), so I will try to focus more on Esau ...and you can read what Max says about Jacob. Though I do know the story is mostly about Jacob, and one cannot separate the two ...so, I will not try.

Max's book, *'Help Is Here'* ...also challenged me to do a little more thinking, which may apply here. Everyone that I heard speak of the study commented that they loved the analogy of 'powerboat' faith compared to 'rowboat' faith.

From what we read about Jacob, it could be said he had 'rowboat' faith ...and maybe at times even 'broken oar' faith.

Way back when I was in college ...I had a couple Social Studies classes that gave us students a view (their view) of the outside world. But, mostly I was not in touch with the outside world because I had to reduce my world to the book in front of me. I was trying to make the grade.

But, after college I had to go out into the world to get a job ...and new worlds came to me. One world was church ...and another one was TV. Often there was an overlap there because people at church recommended things, and work also pushed the idea of "you gotta check this out!"

The church and TV overlap showed enthusiastic energy funneled into what many called the *Faith Movement*, or another called *Word of Faith Movement*. And as you can see, the focus was on *'Faith'.*

What Christian would not want more faith?

Of course, much of the focus was on those who claimed to *'have a corner on the market'.* And I could not relate to these 'showmen', but many others aspired to what was being presented to them ...as a *'greater faith'.*

I just settled for the fact that I didn't have much faith ...yet, I was firm with my belief in God, and was content with that.

Also around that time, John Trent and Gary Smalley published a cute children's book, *'The Treasure Tree'* ...which aimed at helping children understand different personality types, and how we can appreciate each others' strengths. At church, I remember a test was given for the benefit of the adults also. And I clearly recall how people commented, *"I knew she was a lion."*

The personality traits were 'Lion' ...'Beaver' ...'Golden Retriever' ...and 'Otter'. The ones who seemed to be most vocal about how they scored were the 'Golden Retrievers', but I thought 'Lions' were the ones traveling in a ...'pride'.

It seems we have too much of an inclination of labeling ...whether ourselves or others. And it became popular to take these tests. I've also seen one that says they will test to see what Disney character you are most like. And they aren't very accurate ...as I believe most people would be like Pinocchio. Who doesn't lie once in a while to make themselves look better?

But, the Associate Pastor of the church I go to has said, *"It's good to pretend ...because after a while you may get it right."* And I never thought of it that way, but perhaps if Pinocchio can become a *real boy*, each of us can likewise hope to become a *real* Christian.

The most thorough test I took was rather long ...about one hundred questions, and it was rather confusing too. But, I guess that was the point ...because if you don't know what they are driving at, then you can't as easily steer it the way of your preference. You may get closer to where the *'rubber meets the road'*.

The test was supposed to show your strengths and weaknesses in reference to spiritual gifts ...yet, I didn't quite see how many of the questions had anything to do with that. And when we finished the lengthy test, we were to check out our scores.

I didn't believe my score ...so, I rechecked it because I felt I added my score wrong. And I am rather good with mathematics, so to think I added wrong really showed my disbelief with my score results.

I scored very high in the category of 'faith' and second highest in the category of 'discernment'. The feeling that I didn't have much faith was so strong that my discernment also went to the wayside. And I added my score again. But, I came up with the same score for the third time.

I still did not accept the results, so I went back to the test again, and searched for every individual question which was designated to be associated with *faith* in the answer key. And I had to do that twice too.

What I realized at that point was that those 'showmen' who claimed to have a *'corner on the market'* in faith ...were demonstrating a bit of something that made me feel something was not right. Why were these people *'naming'* and *'claiming'* what God was going to do, instead of trusting whatever God chooses to do??

I know it is not 'cut and dried' how everything should be ...and one could say, *"You are just having 'faith' in that test because you like the results."*

But, you just read how I didn't trust the results ...and by finally doing a bit of 'discerning' (with the test key), I realized that having faith in God is believing *God is God*, no matter what happens.

Listen to the lyrics of Steven Curtis Chapman's song: *'God is God'.*

God is who He is ...and not limited to my thoughts, whims, or who I'd like Him to be (and do for me).

It just so happens that I like who the Bible says He is.

I feel God loves us, and wants us to know who He is. And since I feel He would have made that clear—-giving people a written record of what He wants them to know—-then that written record must be around somewhere for people to find.

And it so happens God's Word isn't just somewhere ...it's throughout the entire world.

I still do not claim to have 'powerboat' faith ...let that claim remain with the 'showmen'. As they motor around the lake, they may be sending waves to nearly tip my boat. But, I will row along with Jacob, and we will take turns using the broken oar. Then we will find a spot to reflect and anchor a few thoughts. When that guy motors past, I don't know if it scares the fish or how many it injures ...but, he is not the guy I want to be.

Some of us like the flashy lure thrown in front of us.

Some of us want a safety net, not to be caught off guard ...and others are cautious of that *line* they are fed.

Do we remain in the dark at the bottom? The *bottom line* is we all need love and acceptance.

It is so much easier to accept the truth when you feel accepted for who you are. Then you can better become *a better you*. And I think it is better to let people know Jesus is waiting to accept them ...by wanting them to accept His love and His eternal promises.

Though I am not one of those 'name-it claimers' ...well, I'm also not claiming my analogy is good, or that my life is.

God is good.

Me? I'm just expressing some of my experiences. I wasn't drawn to Jesus by someone *motoring* their slick slogans, catchy convictions, and knighted knowledge *around my peaceful spot* where I listen, waiting for God to touch my heart.

Who is the wisest fisherman (in Luke 5:1-7) that we can read about? Who calmly sat down in the boat, and talked to the people?

I am touched by the quiet, and often hurting hearts ...and I also feel I should not scare the fish, but be a fisher of men (and women).

XVI.

This is the way I see it ...sort of a summary.

I would guess Esau didn't feel loved because he was making decisions that were very much against what his parents (and God) would have for him. Jacob likely didn't feel loved because there was this sense of favoritism where he felt Dad loved his brother more.

With Isaac's two sons ...some may have considered Jacob a 'mama's boy'. It should not really be looked at that way. Every child is *mama's* and *papa's* ...and each parent has something to offer, and that love should be mutual between parent and child.

Some things don't change, and maybe they shouldn't be expected to. Parents are not a different breed from their offspring. All parents are flawed people ...just like the rest of us. And it's not wrong to relate more to one's own interests, yet we can make more of an effort to show interest in things we perhaps are not wholeheartedly interested in. It may be true that we favor one thing over another, but that should not translate into favoring one person over another.

In my family, Dad would be talking about sports and us five boys would enter the intense conversation, yet my lone sister would sit there with her repertoire of different skills and she was a 'straight A' student ...yet, she had little to say about sports. She could have concluded that our conversations were rather petty, and had no real desire to be a part of all that back-and-forth—-but being a part of something is often very important—-no matter what that something is. And like I said, my sister was skilled ...and sharp. And often *actions speak louder than words*. My sister sort of put us in our place when we all played 'Trivial Pursuit All-Star Sports Edition'. And those smiles of satisfaction from Dad and Mom are often all that are needed. I guess my sister was quietly paying attention ...and there is an advantage to that. And my sister is so smart that she retains information unbelievably well.

Some things are clearly remembered, and maintain a very distinct impression—-though that impression is *not* always the same from person-to-person.

Impressions can be entirely different.

Usually that is summed up by saying everyone is different ...we are all just 'wired' slightly different. And most people would not have a problem with this statement.

Did I already say that? With me, it's hard to say ...or perhaps said too easily. But I did say this was a summary.

But how do we view God?

God is the same always, and He loves us all the same.

Perhaps there are those of us who don't understand *that* because we haven't had help understanding it.

When people are still struggling and those attempting to help them haven't had victory over their own struggles, well, sometimes you just have a large knit group of confused people.

XVII.

Growing up, I was given a good wholesome moral upbringing ...and there is no doubt that I was loved. I was also told about God.

And I believed what I was told about God ...and I still do.

Of course, my reading the Bible has been a tremendous help in developing a relationship with Him that has deepened my love and understanding of God.

Family members can bless us in so many ways ...but sadly there are not just one kind of 'people' in this world, and some are conflicted. Worse yet, some people are abusive toward their children. I had the opportunity to work with some of those children at the mental health facility. The government had not yet made a firm stance against it, so I gave some of the children Bibles. I had their name engraved in gold on the cover of the Bible ...to personalize it. And I wholehcartedly hope those children realize how much God *personally* loves them, and that they don't view their Heavenly Father in the same way they view their earthly dad.

Sometimes we are so hurt, we become numb ...and we don't even seek out the truth. We feel there is no understanding that can heal the hurt. We may not even want to talk about it ...because we feel it just makes it worse.

When we close ourselves off from others because we feel we've been hurt in the past, the healing is also closed off. And there is no reason and no understanding.

But, I will try again ...

In Ephesians 1:18, we read: *" ...the eyes of your understanding being enlightened; that you may know what is the hope of His calling, what are the riches of the glory of His inheritance in the saints ..."*

And ...

1 Peter 1:3-4, says: *"Praise be to the God and Father of our Lord Jesus Christ! In His great mercy He has given us new birth into a living hope through the resurrection of Jesus Christ from the dead, and into an inheritance that can never perish, spoil or fade. This inheritance is kept in heaven for you ..."*

If someone dies, and we are left an inheritance ...it may give us temporary joy, not over the death, but from the acknowledgment that someone cared enough to consider us.

Jesus was crucified and died ...and He has you directly in mind, wanting you to join in the joy of the promise of *eternally being with Him*, spared from having to live the next life like this one. That is the richness of His blessing to us …not just to the firstborn, but extended to all of us. That is the inheritance that we can all share in.

There is a slogan that says, *"It's the gift that keeps on giving."* It's a nice saying, but it is only true in reference to the inheritance Jesus offers us. It absolutely keeps on …because it is an *eternal* promise.

To be truly blessed is to realize and accept the *inheritance* Jesus is offering us. And I cannot imagine anyone not wanting that.

I certainly want it for you.

But I can't give it to you …I can only tell you who is offering it to you, and eagerly hope you accept it. I would love to see the joy on your face.

And I hope to see you in Heaven, but for now I will try to find some measure of contentment in knowing that you can also know. There is nothing on earth that is more important, and though I am not the best at communication …there's no activity that is worth my while more than trying to share this with you.

I was thinking how best to finish this …but, it has already been finished. Jesus finished it by His crucifixion, that cruel and torturous death which He endured because *He loves you and me.*

I know it.

I hope you know it too.

$$1$$

$$2$$

$$3$$

$$4$$

$$5$$

$$6$$

$$7$$

$$8$$

$$9$$

$$10$$

I was told that if I *'count to ten'* ...I would not be so anxious??

Actually, I've been counting way too much lately ...as I've been counting here to try to make the spacing better with my words on each line. Who really believes in that *'counting'* anyway ...perhaps taking deeper breaths will work? Maybe not.

These spaces are what authors often use to allow you to write your own comments, but it is a bit distracting to me when it's right in the Chapters, so I'm choosing *not* to do it that way.

I've written two other books involving my study of the Bible:

Chain-Link Fences

We Should Also Love One Another

I began writing while I was in a mental health facility. I worked with preteens and teens. I did my best to treat them fair. There were those who had rarely been treated fairly, and others were there because they treated others unfairly. I showed them both that I cared. The ones who had mostly been treated unfairly seemed to appreciate it more. One who had joined the ranks of those who treated others unfairly—-and didn't want anyone to get in his way when he was doing that—-told me once, "I like it when you aren't working, but I have to admit you treat everyone fair."

Yes, most of them seemed to recognize it when someone really cared, but I felt a bit helpless that I couldn't do more to help them. Yet, I certainly was not for outright interference with their treatment or with their families. Sometimes we need to let them work certain things out for themselves.

Families are important. And often you have to resolve to have family *'come over'* to *overcome* family ...the family struggles, that is.

One boy cried on many occasions when he looked forward to going home on the weekends, and he would wait and wait, until realizing they weren't going to pick him up. He said he was abused by his dad, but he said he learned how to hide when his dad got like that ...and he still wanted to be at home. Always one of the biggest hopes for these kids is that things will get better. And I tend to disagree with many occasions where there is outside interference when there is no physical abuse. The kids may want it to be worked out, otherwise they often don't get over it, and sadly it is also true that they can become just like their dad ...if they are not afforded the opportunity to work it out.

And there are *no* set ways how kids choose to cope. Sometimes they look to TV, and can relate to the *drama and hope* that is often written within the script. One scrawny little boy who I was working with was hard to figure out. He would not open up about anything that was bothering him. We shared the same first name, yet not much else was shared ...but I didn't need to be told that he'd been through a lot of difficulty in his young life. I felt sorry for all of the kids ...and this youngster who would one day be a young man was no exception.

Little Stephen would get frustrated, lower his head, furrow his brow, and puff up his cheeks. Then he'd raise his head and look straight at you with a determined look with his big wide eyes, "I'm going to explode ...you wouldn't like me when I'm angry!"

And I knew he wasn't going to explode with anger, nor was I going to suggest that he *'count to ten'*. I knew the second part of what he said was from the TV show *'The Incredible Hulk'*. And I knew he just wanted to rise above the situation ...where no one could hurt him, and when it would be all over, he could find a quiet place by himself where he could *become himself* again.

We may think we don't like ourselves at times, but we are who we are and we do care about ourselves to the extent that we are not happy with ourselves ...because the 'ourselves' that we are trying to deny, at this moment, all those cumulative 'ourselves' do care enough to be unsatisfied. Yes, God loves all of us ...and the part He would most prefer we change is the negative perceptions of ourselves.

What I decided to do ...is write a book that I thought may relate to their problems. I wanted to write it at their level ...which perhaps was working out okay because writing was not one of my strong points in school (which you could have probably guessed) and so maybe, in fact, I am writing almost up to their level.

And I started with the book, *'So Loved ...'*

I got a positive response from several of them, and one girl felt I was writing about her life ...and though I didn't know about her life, it seemed many of them were going through similar hardships and often abuse in their lives.

That one girl's response was somewhat encouraging ...as I'd wanted to find a way that I could help them more.

My parents also read the book ...and they said they didn't like *the mending*.

I've just written how parents can have an effect upon lives, and in this book I tried to show that with Esau and Jacob. What effect did my parents have on me at that moment? Well, I rewrote *the ending*.

And by rewriting the ending, it did not really end. I felt my ending became too long (who would have guessed that), so I made it into two more books:

The Curious Whether and How

Do the Birds in the Wilderness, Not Heard, Stop Singing Their Songs?

Then my next concern was not to just attempt to relate to their life here on earth and perhaps help them cope ...but to help understand a bit about the purposes and reasons of life itself. And that is always more difficult to understand ...unless we consider God.

And we should not get distracted by any change in the 'climate'. There is a saying, *"When it rains, we do what they did in the old country ...we let it rain."* Now, I'm not going to get into a debate at this time about acid rain or how pollution is having an effect upon our environment (which none of us want) or the inconsistencies of how we seem okay with sending our businesses to areas with little or no regulations (who pollute more). The latest is how hot last year was ...though I know that's a concern, I'm not trying to be insensitive when I say we had a nice mild summer in Michigan here last year. I'm just saying, "We can always do like they did in the old country ...move!"

And don't move to Mars ...there are no *Mars bars* there.

Pastor Myron and I are not going ...there is no chocolate.

And besides, we believe that the earth will not become unlivable as a result of our destroying the planet in that way ...it will become nearly unlivable because it will become like in the time of Noah. Don't quote me on that ...Jesus said it in Matthew 24:37.

And at the time of God's choosing, the old earth will pass away. The new earth will be a new Jerusalem, a city unlike the cities we are used to ...and it will be nearly 2 million square miles.

The Book of Revelation 21:27 says, *"Nothing impure will ever enter it, nor will anyone who does what is shameful or deceitful, but only those whose names are written in the Lamb's book of life."*

Is that scary ...because deep down we know we are helpless to try to save our planet, and we are so distracted that at the same time we are destroying the moral climate? [Somehow that definition, including the word *'moral'* has also changed, to sometimes mean something which seems a bit immoral. But, I'll leave that statement up to Isaiah (5:20). It's actually up to God, yet isn't that what prophets of old did ...speak what God would have them say??]

And each day, I read of those who are trying to convince us that the Bible is no longer relevant, it's outdated, and it's inaccurate. Yet, if we don't trust God's Word, or believe it's God's Word, then how can we trust who God is??

And with that ...we lose our focus.

We need to focus on Jesus ...on what He said, what He did for us, and on His promises to us. Then the truth of the Book of Life is not scary, but comforting.

This is what I believe ...and I believe in the Creation of the world, not the evolution of it and of human beings. And I feel that's important for me to share, so that's why I wrote the book:

The Evolution of Confusion

And you guessed it—-it was too long. Not just too long for my liking or yours—-it was too long for the publisher I was considering going with. And that is actually a good thing, as it does seem better to have a shorter book. And it's easier to manage.

So, I managed to split that book into 5 parts:

1 of 5 'The Essence ...'

2 of 5 'Inevitable Outcome?'

3 of 5 'Train Up a Child ...'

4 of 5 'Where From Here?'

5 of 5 'We Should Know ...'

So, that sort of explains that.

Then I wanted to discuss some things about the Bible, and also list some of my 'short stories'—-*Chain-Link Fences*.

I was content, and thought I was done ...until *'We Should Also Love One Another'*. And what you're reading, plus—-*'What is His Name?'*

And now ...time to work on my Metadata, so I can get *this* book soon into print. (...& preview *'Am I Trying to Take Away From Jesus?'*)

* * * *** * * *

*** * * * 2025, now add *Questions of the Heart* * * * ***

* * *** * *** * *

On the cover of this book, there's an oval portrait of Dad's parents. Dad was the 'firstborn' son ...the center-right photo.

Dad was born in the *much celebrated* 'Roaring Twenties' ...and his parents were hard-working farmers, who didn't do much 'roaring'. Also, most of them didn't own machinery that *roared* either. They had horses to plow a field, a barn full of milk cows, chickens, pigs, and sheep. Of course, before the end of that roaring decade the *Great Depression* hit. And Dad was about 6 years old when it hit its peak.

He had followed his dad everywhere and learned most everything he had to learn about farming. At this young age, after his dad had plowed the field with a team of horses, he was given the task of taking that same team to work the field further with a spring-tooth drag. During the Depression, few people could get much money ...so they couldn't spend much money. And keeping a farm up in good working condition does cost. So what does one do? It's difficult to speak of what everyone would do, but his dad got an extra job skidding logs.

There was much farming in the area, but in the mid-1800s Michigan led all states in timber production ...and it was still going strong at this time. Another reason for small towns dotting the landscape was the iron ore mining industry. And over a dozen miles away, my Mom was being born at this time. There was much shaft and tunnel mining going on, and I remember Mom showing me a structure that had once been the Aragon Iron Mine (not to be confused with 'Aragorn' from *Lord of the Rings*). Her mom told her not to go near there because with so many underground tunnels, who knows when one could collapse or cave in.

One year my Dad's dad got pleurisy and double-pneumonia ...and my Dad and his mom had to take care of most of the farm chores during that time. Times were challenging, but they did what they had to do.

Dad took responsibility for many things as a preteen that most of the teens today would not imagine doing. Is this just one of those *'walking 5 miles uphill against the wind, both ways'* (to and from school) stories? No, it's not ...work on the farm was truly hard. And Dad was *'farm strong'*.

Both Dad and Mom were also being raised in families with a *strong* moral resolve ...and would later pass that on to us.

Work was hard and never-ending. Though something else sadly soon also appeared to be never-ending, as World War 2 would become the worst evil imagined.

Dad had just graduated from High School, had turned 18 years of age in October, and was being shipped out in December. Key industries and some jobs such as baking, farming, medicine, and engineering were often considered 'essential' and those people could be considered exempt from being drafted. When my Dad got drafted, his dad said he could possibly qualify as being exempt ...as he was needed on the farm. But, Dad saw many young men his age having to go ...and he told his dad, "I am *no better* than anyone else, so I will go."

Of course, I am biased ...but, I do consider Dad *better*. I could not think of a better Dad that God could have given me. God didn't give me a perfect dad (and I don't think one exists), but He gave me a real Dad ...one who stood beside Mom, and together they both showed us six children how much we meant to them.

I was not the 'firstborn' ...no, I was born approximately 14 months after my brother. Then a couple years later came my sister, and the following years three more brothers were born.

Unless you know Mom, you will probably not be able to find her in the collage 'within the collage' to the left on this book cover. You can choose to know Mom by how I am going to describe her. She played a very significant role in our family besides merely giving birth to us.

Dad and Mom both agreed that the most significant role she could have was being a stay-at-home Mom. And her loving guidance had a huge positive impact upon our lives. She also took us all to church on Sundays, and I know her heart's desire was for us to understand our inheritance as children of God. But, I wouldn't expect you to really know how special Mom was ...merely by hearing me say she was. Though there *are* many people within the small town I grew up in who would testify to what I'm saying.

What I'm saying about Dad & Mom may be a bit more clear than what I'm saying about the Bible. At times the words and many of the New Testament phrases that the apostles used may be a bit difficult to understand. How does one describe something that many others have not experienced? Yet, you can read how really committed they were—-and if we try to commit just a little bit to seeing the true character of those who were reaching out to the sick, the blind, and downtrodden—-then we may be able to trust the words of those who performed the good works. And the good works were done by mere common folk (and many fishermen) who would not commonly communicate with anyone, unless it was unavoidable. But, they could not refrain from telling others about Jesus and His promises to us.

The disciples of Jesus got to experience something that is so great, we can only get a glimpse of it by reading what they said about Him. Yet, there were wars back then too ...and some of the worst were those which should not even have existed. We could say that no wars should exist, but the outward struggles begin with inward conflicts ...yes, within ourselves. And the disciples began to understand that the outward struggles would never end ...yet what they wanted for the people was to at least have some inner relief, a peace that is not imagined, but which they found to be real. And it was so real that many of them ended up being—-what some perceived as a defeated bunch of losers—-because many of them died while believing in what they believed. Yet, other believers did not give up either ...they continued on telling others about Jesus.

I believe 'love' never gives up ...in its truest sense. And I understand that. What I don't understand is how something that is clearly evil can gain so much support. And that evil seems to find its way into the confused and wayward minds of people who also just don't seem to give up.

If you put together a bunch of preschool kids, teaching them to share: they will smile, laugh, and play together. If you teach them that others are bad, and to not become friends with certain kids—-then there will always be conflict, they'll hold grudges, and 'get even' when they feel they've been wronged—-and they will continually fight. And if someone tries to stop them from fighting, they will just feel they've been wronged again ...and again.

And if they are told their 'Supreme' Teacher/Leader/'Being' supports this ...they'll strive to live for the only affirmation they know.

However our 'Supreme Being' may be viewed, clearly it *isn't* the same throughout the world. One brave person I've listened to on the news said he was raised in one such family—-and he was somehow able to see through the propaganda and hypocrisy—-and see where there is true goodness in the world, a perception of goodness that his dad's 'supreme being' would *never support*. So, how then would it exist if *not tolerated* by his dad's perceived 'supreme being'??

It wouldn't ...

But, that goodness does exist.

Our *Supreme Being* prefers not to eliminate ...but to encourage, convince, give second chances (or seventy times seven), and to do good. We co-exist because our God wants us to.

I know I'm being a bit vague with that ...but, I'll try to present a milder or lighter example that may help you understand the dark dilemma.

So, I will use one more example of something you may possibly be familiar with.

I haven't had any venison for quite some time, but I just had some chocolate, so I'll go with that one.

The original 'Willy Wonka' movie came out while I was in High School in 1971, and there've been a couple others throughout the years. The only other one I saw was last year ...but, I am referencing the original here, which has become a classic.

For those who remember the first one, the 'Golden Ticket' was a very cherished item. But, there were only 5 of them. You had to purchase a Wonka Bar, and unwrap it to see if you had one of the very elusive 'Golden Tickets'.

What if you didn't purchase a Wonka Bar—-someone gave it to you—-and it had a 'Golden Ticket'??

If you told someone how you didn't purchase it—-that it was given to you, then there is a chance that someone may think it was a scam *(remember, I talked about scams at the start of this book)*. And they may further wonder if all of the 5 'Golden Tickets' were given to exactly who Willy Wonka wanted them to go to—-and those 5 kids may have been unfairly selected in advance *(don't you wonder how Wonka's assistant, posing as his nemesis 'Slugworth' was always there when all of the 'Golden Tickets' were found—-the first in Germany; the next in the United Kingdom; the third in Miles City, Montana; the fourth in Marble Falls, Arizona; and 'Charlie' being the fifth, running back home with the ticket and being cut off in an alley by Wonka's assistant?)*. I would certainly be a bit suspicious.

But what if the scenario was different—-and every Wonka Bar had a 'Golden Ticket', and you didn't even have to purchase one—-they were handing them out 'free'. All you had to do is hold onto the 'Golden Ticket' until a time (TBA) ...'to be announced'. And then you could get an unlimited supply of the chocolatey goodness.

I have a friend who is allergic to chocolate, so that would *not* be any bit of 'good news' to him. But, suppose there is more than just chocolate—-there's 'goodness' all around—-in every shape and form.

Is there someone who is allergic to 'goodness'??

If you can't stand any 'goodness' at all, and you favor being around deception—-and think you are the king of it—-you aren't.

The king of deception tells you to reject the goodness of God. It doesn't matter how you reject it—-it could be that you don't believe in God; or you don't believe in who the Bible says He is; or you may believe in a general sense of the 'human intellect'. Or rather you may think the mere *will to survive* will help you to evolve to a higher level of morality—-though whatever that is, it is blind to all the things it chooses to be blind to, while justifying its redefining *'morality'*.

Do we *not* see that 'goodness' does *not* last when we reject Him who is 'good'??

I believe in an afterlife with Him ...the inheritance He offers.

Perhaps you also see it this way ...perhaps not.

I can't imagine what it would be like without Him ...or maybe I can.

And I do *not* say that without a sense of *much sadness*.

All I have to do is look at what is around me which clearly does *not* involve His guidance. And I know I have not seen the worst that there is. But, I know enough to know there is evil.

And I know many things masquerade as 'good' ...yet, I am not going to blame 'goodness' based on the false representation of it.

In the 'Chocolate Factory' there was 'goodness' in all shapes and all sizes, and in the world there is too.

But, evil also comes in all shapes and sizes—-and it's not really particular who it is perpetrated against—-though it does seem to prefer the helpless and often defenseless.

I hope you all seek out the 'goodness' of God.

Yet, I want to be clear ...who among us actually feels they know the true purpose for their life?

Jesus turned over the tables outside of the temple where there was commercial activity taking place. Today, there are occasions where somewhat questionable activity is even *inside of* our churches.

Jesus instructed His disciples to spread the Gospel, the *'good news'*. If we consider ourselves followers of Jesus, why would we not also want to share *who* He is and *what* He has done?? One would think such news would be welcomed ...and life-changing.

So, yes our *'calling'* is to tell others about Jesus. Yet, too often we go way beyond that ...and at times we even try to get involved in what is not our business. Yes, we are to share what the Bible says, but too often we get into the 'judgment' part, as if we have knowledge of when God is going to extend His 'grace'. Or we think He won't because we don't.

Yet again, we would not want to join those who try to change what Jesus has said ...attempting to create an image of Him different from what the Bible says.

And it seems perhaps that is where we should focus our thoughts. Do we want to stand with the Bible's representation of Jesus? Do we want to create our own? Or do we stand in opposition to Jesus, and stand with those who oppose Him?

Jesus wants to be in our lives now, and doesn't it make good sense that if we want to be with Him for eternity (in Heaven), then we should want Him in our lives now also??

I hope so, I sincerely *do* hope that is something you'd all consider.

Jesus didn't have to come to our earth, but He did ...not to save our planet, but to save our hearts.

Jesus knew He was going to go through a horrific crucifixion, but willingly chose to submit to the unimaginable cruelty and torture.

Why?

Because He loves us.

Will you willingly accept His love?

God bless you all ...